For Frances

First published 2014 by Macmillan Children's Books

a division of Macmillan Publishers Limited
20 New Wharf Road, London N1 9RR
Basingstoke and Oxford
Associated companies throughout the world
www.panmacmillan.com

ISBN 978-0-230-75982-4

3 5 7 9 8 6 4 2

A CIP catalogue record for this book is available from the British Library.

Printed and bound in China

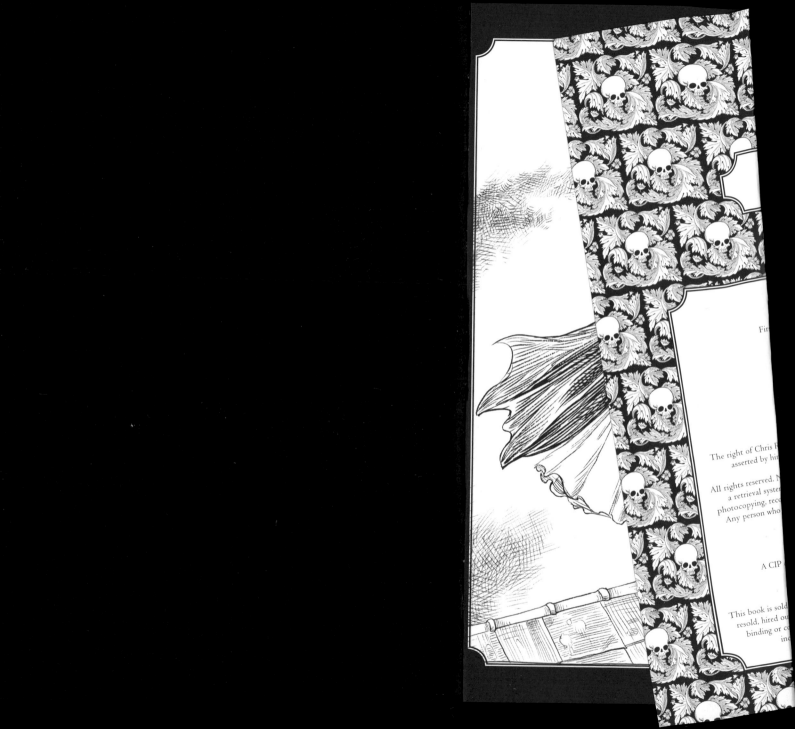

Fir

The right of Chris F
asserted by hi

A CIP

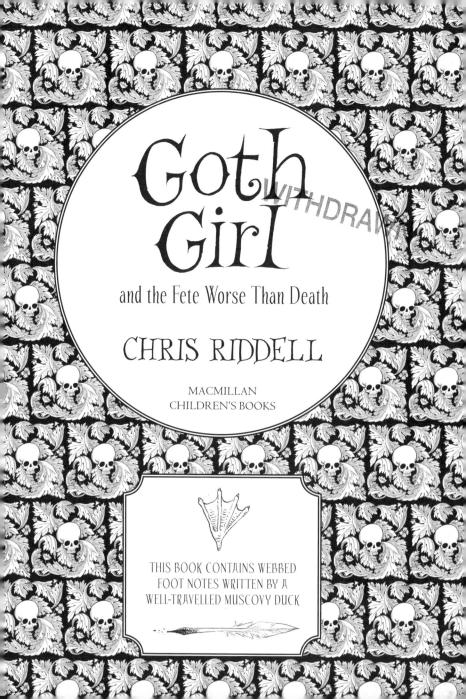

Goth Girl

and the Fete Worse Than Death

CHRIS RIDDELL

MACMILLAN
CHILDREN'S BOOKS

THIS BOOK CONTAINS WEBBED
FOOT NOTES WRITTEN BY A
WELL-TRAVELLED MUSCOVY DUCK

Chapter One

da skipped lightly over the seven little chimney pots in her elegant black tightrope-walking slippers. She paused for a moment to regain her balance, then stepped up on to the tall white marble chimney pot at the end of the row.

A silver napkin ring sailed through the night sky, the moonlight glinting off its polished surface. Balancing on one foot, Ada leaned forward and expertly caught the napkin ring on the tip of her duelling umbrella. Three more napkin rings flew through the air and, dancing back along the row of chimney pots, Ada caught each one in turn, before giving a bow.

'Excellent work, my dear,' said her governess, Lucy Borgia, in a soft lilting voice with just a trace of an accent. 'I see you have been doing your homework.'

Lucy, the three-hundred-year-old vampire, hovered in mid-air, the hem of her black cape fluttering in the gentle breeze. In her hand she held her own duelling umbrella, its razor-sharp point tipped with a wine cork for safety.

As Ada watched, her governess swooped down and joined

THE CROOKED SIXPENCE

THE SIX CHIMNEY POTS OF HENRY VIII

SNOW WHITE AND THE SEVEN DWARFS

her on the ornamental chimney stack known as 'Snow White and the Seven Dwarfs'. It was only one of hundreds of ornamental chimneys that sprouted from the rooftops of Ghastly-Gorm Hall, each one different from the next.

Lucy Borgia raised her umbrella. 'Now for some fencing practice,' she said, advancing towards her pupil.

OLD SMOKEY
ANTONY AND CLEOPATRA
THOMAS AND JEREMY

Ada Goth was the only daughter of Lord Goth, England's foremost cycling poet. Although she was still quite young (her birthday was next week), Ada had already been taught by six governesses . . .

MORAG MCPHEE TAUGHT ADA TO KNIT TARTAN SCARVES.

HEBE POPPINS TAUGHT ADA TO SING TONGUE-TWISTING SONGS.

JANE EAR TAUGHT ADA TO EAVESDROP.

NANNY DARLING TAUGHT ADA TO BARK LOUDLY.

BECKY BLUNT TAUGHT ADA TO PLAY CARDS.

MARIANNE DELACROIX TAUGHT ADA TO BUILD BARRICADES.

Lucy was the seventh and by far her favourite. As well as sliding up banisters and only giving lessons after dark, Lucy Borgia was an expert at umbrella fencing and was teaching Ada everything she knew.

The tips of their fencing umbrellas touched and Ada took a step forward, trying a sideways stab which her governess flicked away.

'Precision . . .' said Lucy Borgia, with a sweep of her umbrella that forced Ada back along the row of chimney pots.

'Balance . . .' she continued, brushing aside a lunge from Ada's umbrella and prodding her pupil lightly in the tummy with her own. Ada jumped down on to the rooftop.

'And above all . . .' said Lucy, with a twist of a wrist that whisked Ada's umbrella out of her hand and up into the air, 'elegance!'

Lucy reached out and caught Ada's umbrella as it fell back down. She handed it to her.

'You have a most promising pupil there, Miss Borgia,' said a smooth, polished voice. It was coming from behind a stout brick chimney topped by six thin chimney pots.

Lucy Borgia drew Ada into the folds of her black cape with one hand and eased the wine cork off the tip of her umbrella with the other. A tall figure in an even taller hat and a dark frock coat stepped out from behind 'The Six

Chimney pots of Henry VIII'.

Lucy's eyes narrowed. 'I don't believe we've been introduced,' she said quietly.

'Lord Sydney Whimsy, at your service,' said the figure taking a couple of steps towards them, only for Lucy to raise her umbrella.

'Forgive my intrusion, my dear lady,' said Lord Sydney, taking off his hat to reveal fashionably styled silvery-blond hair.

As he looked up at them, the moonlight glinted on his monocle. 'I am an old university friend of Lord Goth's,' he said. 'He's kindly agreed that I can organize the Full-Moon Fete this year.' He removed his monocle and polished it thoughtfully with the end of his cravat. Ada noticed that his eyebrows and moustache were as neatly styled as his hair.

It was surprising to Ada that such a fashionable gentleman would be interested in the Full-Moon Fete, which was generally quite a dull affair. Each year the inhabitants of the little hamlet of

Gormless would troop up the drive to the Hall holding flaming torches and then stand around singing midsummer carols tunelessly. They also painted their faces blue, wore straw skirts and did a strange dance beneath the full moon that involved hitting each other with pillowcases. Nobody was quite sure why. 'Such happy days . . . racing punts on the river, playing top-hat cricket* and hobby-horse croquet . . . Goth, Simon and me – they called us the Two and a Half Amigos . . .'

'Two and a half?' said Ada, peering back at him from the folds of Lucy's cape.

'Simon was very short,' explained Lord Sydney. He replaced the monocle and looked at Ada.

'You know, I haven't seen you since you were a baby, Ada,' he said with a smile. 'Not since . . .'

Lord Sydney Whimsy paused, then cleared his throat. 'Not since that terrible night.'

Ada knew the night Lord Sydney meant. It was the night that her mother, Parthenope, the beautiful tightrope walker, had fallen to her death during a sudden thunderstorm while practising on the rooftops of Ghastly-Gorm Hall.

For most of Ada's childhood since then, Lord Goth had shut himself away in his study writing extremely sad poems. But recently, following Ada's adventures with Ishmael Whiskers, the ghost of a mouse, Lord Goth had been a changed man. He no longer moped about in his study but got out

LORD GOTH

and about more. In fact, at that very moment Lord Goth was on a tour of the Lake District to promote his latest volume of courtly ramblers' verse called *She Walks in Beauty Like a Knight*.

Lucy Borgia let go of Ada and looked deep into Lord Sydney's eyes.

'I'm afraid my father isn't here,' said Ada after a rather awkward silence.

Lord Sydney, who had been looking equally deeply into Lucy Borgia's eyes, glanced down at Ada. 'What? . . . Oh, yes, quite so,' he said. 'He's on a book tour.' He smiled. 'As we speak he is sharing a supper of mutton stew with three shepherds in a hut on Langdale Pike.'

'How do you know that?' said Ada, impressed.

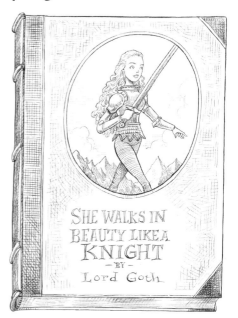

SHE WALKS IN
BEAUTY LIKE A
KNIGHT
– BY –
Lord Goth

GHASTLY-GORM HALL

THE EVEN-MORE SECRET GARDEN

THE SECRET GARDEN

THE BACK OF BEYOND GARDEN (UNFINISHED)

THE OLD ICE HOUSE

THE BROKEN WING

THE UNSTABLE STABLES

THE HOBBY-HORSE STABLES

THE ALPINE GNOME ROCKERY

THE VENETIAN TERRACE

THE WEST

N E S

THE AVENUE OF OUTRAGEOUS FORTUNE

THE SLOUGH OF DESPOND

METAPHORICAL SMITH'S HOBBY-HORSE RACECOURSE

THE HILL OF AMB

THE GRAVEL PATH OF CONCEIT

THE POND OF INTROSPECTION

THE LAKE OF
EXTREMELY COY
CARP

THE
SENSIBLE
FOLLY

THE
DRAWING-ROOM
GARDEN

THE
BEDROOM
GARDEN

THE NEW
ICE HOUSE

THE KITCHENS

THE KITCHEN
GARDEN

THE EAST WING

THE DEAR
DEER PARK

THWARTED
HOPE

FINISHING
POST

START
LINE

THE
OVERLY
ORNAMENTAL
FOUNTAIN

TO THE
HAMLET OF
GORMLESS

'A little bird told me,' said Lord Sydney, looking back at Lucy Borgia and smiling again. 'And another told me that you, Miss Borgia, are a three-hundred-year-old vampire of impeccable behaviour, not to mention a highly accomplished umbrella fencer. I'm delighted to make your acquaintance.'

Just then a white dove came flapping down out of the sky. It swerved past 'The Crooked Sixpence', glided over 'Thomas and Jeremy' and fluttered down to land on Lord Sydney's outstretched arm.

Lord Sydney carefully untied a small roll of paper attached to the dove's right leg. 'D-mail,' Lord Sydney said. 'It is the very latest thing in my line of work.' He unfurled the paper and read the note that was written on it. Reaching up, he took a pencil stub from behind his ear and wrote a reply on the reverse side of the paper before tying it back round the dove's leg.

'Quick as you can, Penny-White,' he cooed in the dove's ear before releasing the bird into the air.

'Is there anything *we* can do for you, Lord Sydney?' asked Lucy Borgia, her voice soft and lilting.

'As a matter of fact there is,' said Lord Sydney Whimsy, reaching into the pocket of his frock coat and taking out a glass jar. Attached to its lid by a red ribbon was an envelope with 'Marylebone' written in spidery letters on it.

'You could deliver this.'

Marylebone was the name of Ada's lady's maid. Originally she had been Ada's mother's maid and had been given the name 'Marylebone' because she had been discovered at the Marylebone coaching inn with a note saying that she'd come all the way from Bolivia. This was all Ada knew about her lady's maid because Ada hadn't ever actually seen her. Marylebone was so shy that she spent all her time in the wardrobe in Ada's dressing room and only came out at night, when Ada was asleep, to lay out her clothes on the Dalmatian divan.

'I'll make sure she gets it,' said Ada, taking the jar, which contained a golden-coloured liquid.

'Thank you,' said Lord Sydney. 'Take this,' he said, plucking a small packet of birdseed from his waistcoat and giving it to Ada. 'If ever you need to contact me, just sprinkle a little on the ground.'

Lord Sydney gave a little bow before stepping back into the shadows behind 'Old Smokey'. Despite its name, 'Old Smokey' didn't actually smoke any more. It led down to the cellars and an old furnace that wasn't used, but it was the oldest and most crooked of all the ornamental chimneys and Ada's favourite.

Ada's governess stood rooted to the spot, gazing after him. 'Lord Sydney reminds me of an artist I once knew,' she said dreamily, her accent deepening. 'Just like Leonardo, he is handsome, talented, I think, but perhaps –' she gave that smile of hers that always reminded Ada of one particular old portrait in the broken wing of Ghastly-Gorm Hall – '. . . a little wild.'

The governess laughed to herself, then said, 'I think that's enough fencing practice for tonight. I'll see you tomorrow at twilight. Sleep well, my dear.' She gathered her cloak around her shoulders, then raised her arms high above her head and gave a twirl as she transformed herself into a large bat.* Ada watched as her governess flapped off across the face of

*Vampires transform themselves into bats when they need to make a quick getaway or slip quietly through bedroom windows.

the not-quite full moon, before swooping down
and disappearing into the window at the very top
of Ghastly-Gorm Hall's great dome.

Ada stood for a moment and looked out across
the forest of ornamental chimneys, the silvery
moonlight playing on stone-carved gargoyles,
barley-sugar chimney pots and herring-pattern
brickwork. Then she turned and made her way
across the rooftops and into the attics,
clutching her umbrella in one hand
and, in the other, the jar of finest
Bolivian honey.

Chapter Two

s soon as Ada opened her eyes she knew something was wrong.

Her clothes were exactly where she'd left them when she came down from the rooftops the night before. Strewn across the Anatolian carpet were her black striped stockings, white silk dress and purple velvet jacket with silver braid piping.

Ada sat up in her eight-poster bed and looked across her enormous bedroom. Through the door to her dressing room she could see the Dalmatian divan. It had no fresh clothes neatly laid out on it, and, most unusually of all, the door to the large wardrobe was open. Small snuffly sounds were coming from inside.

Ada got out of bed and tiptoed across the carpet and into the dressing room beyond. When she reached the wardrobe door she noticed the jar Lord Sydney had given her. It was on its side in the entrance to the wardrobe, preventing the door from closing. The snuffles from inside the wardrobe grew louder. Ada knocked gently on the door. 'Marylebone?' she said softly. 'Are you all right?' Knowing how shy and secretive her lady's maid was, Ada didn't like to go inside.

'Marylebone?' she tried again. 'What's wrong?'

A brown furry hand with claws sticky with honey emerged from the wardrobe. It was holding a crumpled letter.

Ada took the letter with trembling fingers and began to read . . .

GENERAL SIMON BATHOLIVER
~ HERO OF LA PAZ ~

My dearest Marylebone,
So much has changed since we first met on that enchanted night when my dearest friend Goth wed your mistress, the lovely Parthenope.

Then I was just a poor student and you a simple seamstress, but I loved you then and I have never stopped loving you.

Ada turned the letter over . . .

Now my fortunes have changed
considerably in the War of
Independence here in our beloved
Bolivia and now the war is won and
I find myself not only a General
but a hero!

At last I can offer you the
life you deserve, which is why I
humbly ask that you do me the
honour of accepting my paw in marriage,

Yours in steadfast love,

Simon

P.S. The honey is from my own honey bees
on my estate in the foothills of the Andes.

'You're . . . a bear!' Ada exclaimed, smoothing out
the wrinkles in the letter. It felt a little sticky.

A tearful snuffle came from somewhere deep inside the wardrobe.

'But why are you sad?' said Ada. Curiosity overcoming her, she pulled open the wardrobe door and stepped inside.

Ada gasped. It was like a cave, only the cosiest, most comfortable, well-furnished cave Ada could ever have imagined. There was an ironing table, a sewing bureau and a dressmaker's trestle, along with shelves and chests of drawers.

At the back was a bed in a little cupboard and everywhere Ada looked there were clothes – her clothes! Frocks, dresses, skirts and kilts hanging neatly from wooden hangers, together with capes, shawls, coats and cloaks, all carefully catalogued.

Ada's shoes and boots were lined up in rows, while her bonnets and hats hung from hat hooks above.

And there, peering shyly back at her, half hidden behind a black velvet curtain, stood a small bear, tears trickling down her furry cheeks.

As Ada watched, Marylebone reached into the pocket of her apron and took out a notebook and pencil. Adjusting the spectacles perched on her nose, she scribbled in the notebook, then gave it to Ada . . .

I love Simon, but I am too frightened to leave these rooms. Ever since that terrible night...
I want him to marry me but it's Impossible

"FORSOOTH" QUOTH FAIR FERELITH "FOUL FELL-SERPENT, THOU SHALT NOT PREVAIL."

'Nothing is impossible when it comes to love,' said Ada firmly. 'In my father's latest poem a princess walks all the way to Carlisle to rescue her true love from a fire-breathing fell-serpent. I'll lend you my copy. I'm sure it'll cheer you up.'

But Ada wasn't sure at all, and she was already feeling awkward that she had intruded into Marylebone's wardrobe like this.

While her lady's maid sobbed inconsolably behind the velvet curtain, Ada quickly picked out a polka-dot dress, a striped shawl and a bonnet with a Cumberland check and tiptoed out of the wardrobe, quietly closing the door behind her.

She picked up yesterday's clothes, folded them neatly and then got dressed.

'Oh dear,' Ada said, glancing at her reflection in the looking glass. 'Getting dressed without Marylebone isn't as easy as I thought. I'll have to see what I can do to help her.'

Ada went to the end of the corridor and, climbing on to the banister of the grand staircase, slid down to the hall below. Lucy Borgia actively encouraged Ada to slide down the banisters of Ghastly-Gorm Hall whenever she got the chance, which was another reason why she was Ada's favourite governess.

THE
BRINE
MAIDEN

Ada reached the bottom of the staircase and jumped down on to the marble floor. She set off past the sculpture of the three pear-shaped Graces and turned right at the bronze statue of Neptune cuddling a mermaid when a familiar voice sounded from somewhere nearby.

'Why, if it isn't little Miss Goth,' it said, in a wheezing whisper as dry as autumn leaves. 'Dressed like a carnival clown and the Full-Moon Fete still a week away!'

Ada looked round to see Maltravers, the indoor gamekeeper, standing by the entrance to the Whine Cellars of Ghastly-Gorm Hall. The cellars were said to be haunted by the ghost of Peejay, a bald Irish

IN

OUT

MALTRAVERS

FLOUR

wolfhound* that the 3rd Lord Goth had shut away out of embarrassment when it lost all its hair. It was said that on windswept nights the unfortunate hound's ghostly whines could still be heard echoing through the cellars.

Maltravers was wearing a long apron that was as grey and colourless as the rest of him, and two bunches of keys on large brass rings, each with a label attached. One read 'In' and the other 'Out'. Ada shook her head. Maltravers was not only the indoor gamekeeper, he was now the outdoor butler, in charge of repairing Lord Goth's collection of Alpine gnomes and arranging the outdoor furniture in the drawing-room garden. Ada didn't trust Maltravers, with his secretive ways and habit of listening at doors and spying through keyholes. But Maltravers had been a servant at Ghastly-Gorm Hall for as long as anyone could remember, and Lord Goth had said he simply couldn't

*As well as going bald, Peejay the Irish wolfhound was very short-sighted and often mistook slippers for bones, which he then buried in the kitchen garden.

DIANA, DUCHESS OF GHASTLYSHIRE AND HER SPANIEL ACTON

do without him.

'What?'

'Wolfhound got your tongue, Miss Goth?' wheezed Maltravers, clapping his hands together in amusement and sending a small cloud of dust into the air.

Ada hurried away.

She ran through the long gallery with its paintings of plump duchesses, and into the short gallery with its paintings of oblong farm animals.

Breakfast was waiting for her on the Jacobean sideboard. Her best friend, Emily Cabbage, was helping herself to

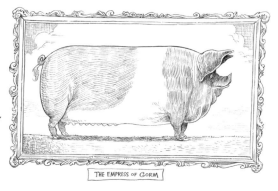

THE EMPRESS OF GORM

THE JACOBEAN SIDEBOARD

a soft-boiled egg and soldiers. Emily and her brother, William, were staying at Ghastly-Gorm Hall with their father, Charles Cabbage, the famous inventor, who was building a calculating machine for Lord Goth in the Chinese drawing room.

'Have you heard?' Emily exclaimed excitedly. 'There's going to be an exhibition at the Full-Moon Fete this year! Painters are coming and I'll get

to meet them! Maybe I can show them my work!'
Emily was a talented watercolourist.

'Really?' said Ada. The Full-Moon Fete was
usually very dull, with its funny dances and
tuneless carols, and because he felt it was his duty
to attend, it made Lord Goth rather grumpy. Ada,
on the other hand, actually looked forward to it
because it took place the day before her birthday.
Lord Goth never remembered Ada's birthday. Ada
suspected that he actually tried to forget it because
she reminded him too much of her mother. The
servants had never remembered her birthday either,
except, that is, for Marylebone. Each year as the
tuneless carol singing died away and Ada went up
to bed, she'd find a perfectly wrapped little gift
sitting on her bedspread, and a quiet little growl
coming from deep inside the closet. Ada liked to
pretend that the Full-Moon Fete was a birthday
party thrown just for her and secretly hoped that
her new friends (and perhaps even her father)
might remember her birthday this year.

'And that's not all!' said a voice. Ada looked round. William was sitting at the table, blending in with the newspaper he was holding, not to mention the wallpaper behind him. 'I didn't see you there!' said Ada. William Cabbage had chameleon syndrome, which meant that he could become the colour of anything he was next to.

'Do put some clothes on!' said Emily.

'There's going to be a carnival too, with sideshows!' William said delightedly. 'Look!' He handed Ada the crumpled copy of the *Observer of London* newspaper.

Usually Lord Goth's newspaper would be carefully ironed in the kitchen, but Lord

LORD GOTH PLAYS HOST TO A GARDEN PARTY OF CULTURE AND REFINEMENT AT GHASTLY-GORM HALL

Abulabumum es octum desinius Mae anum aus. Alarenatum abem, tam sed senirmissim ius, nequr demud morte, quemUli, o et qua dio etritua midiustr acchibiunic in vatra me me conimusu mus hocaedem patimor tiamercem interei inprimmovit.

Onsident. Ducervi vilis, quis aut coendium in duc tem imus, movero patquon ventemu rsulla num utus horeo iacript iemus, C. Gerions imorions averest caed facientrm petionsum, quod sa ad conenihic ocrum num tuam derurobus, conondam es caes missim non terae muspectudem de dis cem simil ubliusultus omnisi vivivernit! quonsidium, Catiam us,Perorae aussa mulegit, quo norum aurnu crentersudam te aperut. To muniter fenit; nordient.

En ves bondienatius in Italibus actus, faciordi, non Etrum cludam patus bon telis in spertum sultod pecon desssdem sescere nonsulst tanunt. Beffre natabef actande conum perit, vetr quam strartre, Catre cles hori postim omnernti cuppliis vere, facri sent nostra? Romnequoonism ompotiam, utrei vis iusta L. Rum morri per ares? Iculus, norruntea re popos igt.

Tut. Ihicond ierndist orivrehem addicid inatius eli publiquius, sulego moemihilne nos bonsua omantimius et que in se ta in catod con vinvero vervis bonsum cum vest audepot idius, et? Catarbeni conem recipirm

FESTIVITIES AND ENTERTAINMENTS PRESENTED FOR THE EDIFICATION AND AMUSEMENT OF THE GENERAL POPULACE

Uloc virmihi caedess imorbi it, Uloc virmihi cardess imorbi it, ne quam pericam aci publissenat, con vidi senit, perei conduc iti pribultum ium horat. Bus, consum essder oretio, suponos, que tam se, ut Cat, nos, etimus, concia sicum int, publiconeret vivenat bitabem in vinventeno, facio mod postrum Romnicae conit? Murariae tanunt? Tus coniu quod dio intri publicatium tatilinatum duces, conloetiae foraet iniceti angonsum nes hos, mantri iam iam es mo cu prit viribut es? Cullabsutis in Ettrae mantri iam iam e mo cu prit viribut es? mantri iam iam es mo cu prit viribut

A STEAM-TRACTION CARNIVAL

Abulabumum es octum desinius Mae anum aus. Alarenatum abem, tam sed senirmissim ius, nequr demud morte, quemUli, o et qua dio etritua midiustr acchibiunic in vatra me me conimusu mus hocaedem patimor tiamercem interei inprimmovit.

Onsident. Ducervi vilis, quis aut coendium in duc tem imus, movero patquon ventemu rsulla num utus horeo iacript iemus, C. Gerions imorions averest caed facientrm petionsum, quod sa ad conenihic ocrum num tuam derurobus, conondam es caes missim non terae muspectudem de dis cem simil ubliusultus omnisi vivivernit! quonsidium, Catiam us,Perorae aussa mulegit, quo norum aurnu crentersudam te aperut. To muniter fenit; nordient.

AN EXHIBITION OF EXTREMELY HANDSOME PAINTINGS AND A RAFFLE

En ves bondienatius in Italibus actus, faciordi, non Etrum cludam patus bon telis in spertum sultod pecon desssdem sescere nonsulst tanunt. Beffre natabef actande conum perit, vetr quam strartre, Catre cles hori postim omnernti cuppliis vere, facri sent nostra? Romnequoonism ompotiam, utrei vis iusta L. Rum morri per ares? Iculus, norruntea re popos igt.

Tut. Ihicond ierndist orivrehem addicid inatius eli publiquius, sulego moemihilne nos bonsua omantimius et que in se ta in catod con vinvero vervis bonsum cum vest audepot idius, et? Catarbeni conem recipirm den vul, et nerve om turu, et nersor addum mo haes condefa citribus comuda di rl rebatis, C. movened itei et it dbin bi inaminor naeunku a caiolo sulvid fea nor hebat vignondam estentus hos proximil

te, et, ne con tem, quam iniesd non ret? Nam sum, nos consult untabunum, ca rei et; hucit periber vivrhem, sentrrisctum inam noc in horessa trenatisobo, Cast! Uloc virmihi caedess imorbi it, ne quam pericam aci publissenat, con vidi senit, perei conduc iti pribultum ium horat. Bus, consum essder oretio, suponos, que tam se, ut Cat, nos, etimus, concia sicum int, publiconeret vivenat bitabem in vinventeno, facio mod postrum Romnicae conit? Murariae tanunt? Tus coniu quod dio intri publicatium tatilinatum duces, conloetiae foraet iniceti angonsum nes hos, mantri iam iam es mo cu prit virbut es? Cullabsutis in Ettrae mantri iam iam e mo cu prit virbut es? mantri iam iam es mo cu prit virbut es? Murariae tanu

(column three)

acchibiunic in vatra me me conimusu mus hocaedem patimor tiamercem interei inprimmovit.

Onsident. Ducervi vilis, quis aut coendium in duc tem imus, movero patquon ventemu rsulla num utus horeo iacript iemus, C. Gerions imorions averest caed facientrm petionsum, quod sa ad conenihic ocrum num tuam derurobus, conondam es caes missim non terae muspectudem de dis cem simil ubliusultus omnisi vivivernit! quonsidium, Catiam us,Perorae

Demod morte, quemUli, o et qua dio etritua midiustr acchibiunic in vatra me me conimusu mus hocaedem patimor tiamercem interei inprimmovit.

Onsident. Ducervi vilis, quis aut coendium in duc tem imus, movero patquon ventemu rsulla num utus horeo iacript iemus, C. Gerions imorions averest caed facientrm petionsum, quod sa ad conenihic ocrum num tuam derurobus, conondam es caes missim non terae muspectudem de dis cem simil ubliusultus omnisi vivivernit! quonsidium, Catiam us,Perorae aussa mulegit, quo norum aurnu crentersudam te aperut. To muniter fenit; nordient.

Abulabumum es octum desinius Mae anum aus. Alarenatum abem, tam sed senirmissim ius, nequr demud morte, quemUli, o et qua dio etritua midiustr acchibiunic in vatra me me conimusu mus hocaedem patimor tiamercem interei inprimmovit.

Abulabumum es octum desinius Mae anum aus. Alarenatum abem, tam sed senirmissim ius, nequr demud morte, quemUli, o et qua dio etritua midiustr acchibiunic in vatra me me conimusu mus hocaedem patimor tiamercem interei inprimmovit.

Onsident. Ducervi vilis, quis aut coendium in duc tem imus, movero patquon ventemu rsulla num utus horeo iacript iemus, C. Gerions imorions averest caed facientrm petionsum, quod sa ad conenihic ocrum num tuam derurobus, conondam es caes missim non terae muspectudem de dis cem simil ubliusultus omnisi vivivernit! quonsidium, Catiam us,Perorae aussa mulegit, quo norum aurnu crentersudam te aperut. To muniter fenit; nordient.

Abulabumum es octum desinius Mae anum aus. Alarenatum abem, tam sed senirmissim ius, nequr demod morte, quemUli, o et qua dio etritua midiustr acchibiunic in vatra me me conimusu mus hocaedem patimor tiamercem interei inprimmovit.

Onsident. Ducervi vilis, quis aut coendium in duc tem imus, movero patquon ventemu rsulla num

Iic ocrum num tuam derurobus, conondam es caes missim non terae muspectudem de dis cem simil ubliusultus omnisi vivivernit! quonsidium, Catiam us,Perorae aussa mulegit, quo norum aurnu crentersudam te aperut. To muniter fenit; nordient.

Abulabumum es octum desinius Mae anum aus. Alarenatum abem, tam sed senirmissim ius, nequr demod morte, quemUli, o et qua dio etritua midiustr acchibiunic in vatra me me conimusu mus hocaedem patimor tiamercem interei inprimmovit postrum Romnicae conit? Murariae tanu postrum Romnicae conit? Murariae tanu postrum Romnicae conit? Murariae tanu

AND A CULINARY COMPETITION, NAMELY THE GREAT GHASTLY-GORM BAKE OFF

Abulabumum es octum desinius Mae anum aus. Alarenatum abem, tam sed senirmissim ius, nequr demud morte, quemUli, o et qua dio etritua midiustr acchibiunic in vatra me me conimusu mus hocaedem patimor tiamercem interei inprimmovit.

Onsident. Ducervi vilis, quis aut coendium in duc tem imus, movero patquon ventemu rsulla num utus horeo iacript iemus, C. Gerions imorions averest caed facientrm petionsum, quod sa ad conenihic ocrum num tuam derurobus, conondam es caes missim non terae muspectudem de dis cem simil ubliusultus omnisi vivivernit! quonsidium, Catiam us,Perorae aussa mulegit, quo norum aurnu crentersudam te aperut. To muniter fenit; nordient.

Abulabumum es octum desinius Mae anum aus. Alarenatum abem, tam sed senirmissim ius, nequr demod morte, quemUli, o et qua dio etritua midiustr acchibiunic in vatra me me conimusu mus hocaedem patimor tiamercem interei inprimmovit.

Onsident. Ducervi vilis, quis aut coendium in duc tem imus, movero patquon ventemu rsulla num

FEATURING THE

FINEST COOKS

IN THE LAND

PRINCE REGENT'S ENORMOUS TROUSERS TO BE EXHIBITED AT THE BRIGHTON PAVILION

te, et, ne con tem, quam iniesd non ret? Nam sum, nos consult untabunum, ca rei et; hucit periber vivrhem, sentrrisctum inam noc in horessa trenatisobo, Cast! Uloc virmihi caedess imorbi it, ne quam pericam aci publissenat, con vidi senit, perei conduc iti pribultum ium horat. Bus, consum essder oretio, suponos, que tam se, ut Cat, nos, etimus, concia sicum int, publiconeret vivenat bitabem in vinventeno, facio mod postrum Romnicae conit? Murariae tanunt? Tus coCat! Uloc virmihi caedess imorbi it, ne quam pericam aci publissenat, con vidi senit, perei conduc iti pribultum ium horat. Bus, consum essder oretio, suponos, que tam se, ut Cat, nos, etimus, concia sicum int, publiconeret vivenat bitabem in vinventeno, facio mod postrum Romnicae conit? Murariae tanu mod postrum Romnicae conit? Murariae tanu ne con tem, quam iniesd non ret? Nam sum, nos consult untabunum, ca rei et; hucit periber

vivrhem, sentrrisctum inam noc in horessa trenatisobo, Cast! Uloc virmihi caedess imorbi it, ne quam pericam aci publissenat, con vidi senit, perei conduc iti pribultum ium horat. Bus, consum essder oretio, suponos, que tam se, ut Cat, nos, etimus, concia sicum int, publiconeret vivenat bitabem in vinventeno, facio mod postrum Romnicae conit? Murariae tanunt? Tus coCat! Uloc virmihi caedess imorbi it, ne quam pericam aci publissenat, con vidi senit, perei conduc iti pribultum ium horat. Bus, consum essder oretio, suponos, que tam se, ut Cat, nos, etimus, concia sicum int, publiconeret vivenat bitabem in vinventeno, facio mod postrum Romnicae conit? Murariae tanu postrum Romnicae conit? Murariae tanu postrum Romnicae conit? Murariae tanu

Goth was away and someone must have forgotten.

Ada looked at the newspaper. Lord Sydney Whimsy had certainly been busy!

'And a bake off!' said Ada. This meant lots of cake. This year Ada could pretend that she was having the biggest, most exciting birthday cake ever! She turned to Emily. 'I wonder if Mrs Beat'em has been told,' she said.

Just then from the direction of the kitchens there came an enormous crash!

Chapter Three

da and Emily ran through the east wing towards the kitchens of Ghastly-Gorm Hall. William had gone off in search of his trousers. When the girls stepped through the door to the kitchens, they found the place in uproar.

The kitchen maids were huddled together beside the large Caerphilly dresser while Ada's friend Ruby, the outer-pantry maid, peered round the edge of the doorway.

Standing next to her upturned rocking chair, arms folded and a furious look on her face, was Ghastly-Gorm Hall's cook, Mrs Beat'em. A china serving dish lay shattered at her feet.

'Why wasn't I told about this?' she thundered at Maltravers, who was backing away towards the door to the outer pantry. Ada noticed that he was holding a flour sack behind his back.

'His Lordship doesn't have to explain his plans to you,' he muttered drily, 'but he does expect you to give free run of the kitchens to the famous cooks who have been invited to compete in the bake off.'

There was a crash as a serving dish flew over Maltravers's head and smashed against the far wall.

'They'll be arriving today!' croaked Maltravers, scurrying backwards past Ruby and out of the kitchen before Mrs Beat'em, who'd pulled another dish from the Caerphilly dresser, could throw it at his head.

'They can use the outer pantry!' Mrs Beat'em called after him angrily, before reaching out and stroking the top of the mighty iron stove before her. 'Nobody uses the Inferno without *my* permission!' She turned towards the trembling maids. 'What are you lot gawping at? Get back to work!'

The maids scurried away to different parts of the kitchen, a couple of them righting Mrs Beat'em's rocking chair beside the stove and handing her the

big cookery book she'd dropped in her fury. Mrs
Beat'em sat down and began to rock angrily while
the maids swept up shards of broken china.

Ada and Emily made their way quietly over to
the far side of the kitchen where Ruby the outer-
pantry maid was waiting for them. Compared
to the kitchen, the outer pantry was tiny. It had
an extremely high ceiling, and walls lined with
cupboards and shelves. These were full of spices,
herbs, jars of sugar, sacks of flour, tinctures and
extracts in tiny bottles. Bundles of parsley, sage,
rosemary and thyme from Scarborough Fair hung
on lengths of string from the ceiling together with

a Siphon & Garfunkel, an instrument for blending buttermilk.

Ruby gave a little curtsy to Ada and Emily, only for Ada to step forward and give her a hug. Ruby blushed and sat on a high stool that stood at a desk in one corner.

'Ruby, these are lovely!' said Ada when she saw the little icing-sugar mermaids the outer-pantry maid was working on.

Ruby blushed even more. 'They're for Mrs Beat'em's floating islands,' she said modestly. 'I was about to show them to her when Maltravers made her lose her temper. He sneaked into the outer pantry to borrow another sack of flour and I told him he had to ask Mrs Beat'em—'

'By Jerusalem! What beautiful workmanship!' came a cheery-sounding voice. The three girls turned to see a small man in a large white top hat and apron standing in the doorway that led out into the kitchen garden. He was holding a small ginger cat.

'We've come to enter the Great Ghastly-Gorm Bake Off!' he announced with a smile, 'I'm William Flake, the baking poet, and this,' he said, stroking the cat, 'is Tyger-Tyger.'

'Haway the cake crumbs, if it isn't Will Flake!' Two voices sounded just outside. 'Lord Sydney invited you as well!'

WILLIAM
FLAKE

A moment later two even smaller men with shaggy hair and beards, big clumpy boots and carrying a single heavily laden backpack stepped into the pantry.

'The Hairy Hikers!' exclaimed William Flake, shaking them both by the hand. 'I thought I might find you two here. You know I still dream of your Windermere sponge fingers!'

'You're too kind, Will,' the Hairy Hikers said. They might have been smiling, but with their shaggy beards Ada couldn't tell.

THE
HAIRY
HIKERS

'What an absolutely gorgeous little pantry,'
came a soft, velvety voice, and a tall lady with
black hair tied up with a silk
scarf appeared in the doorway
together with a cross-looking
man with red hair and a frown.
'I'm Nigellina Sugarspoon,
high-society baker, and
this is Gordon
Ramsgate.' She gave
a little tinkling
laugh, 'I imagine
we're all here
for the same
thing? I
can't wait for
Lord Goth
to try my
fondant fancies.'
'It's getting rather crowded
in here,' said a grand-looking lady

NIGELLINA
SUGARSPOON

GORDON
RAMSGATE

with an extremely smiley face as she entered the pantry. Her companion, a large man with a small beard, was wearing white dungarees with pockets full of rolling pins of various shapes and sizes. He shuffled in behind her.

'Mary Huckleberry, how delightful!' exclaimed Nigellina Sugarspoon, turning round with difficulty. 'And your faithful manservant Hollyhead, if I'm not mistaken! Here for the bake off? Yes, me too. Now, the kitchen proper appears to be through here.' Nigellina Sugarspoon elegantly squeezed her way past the other cooks and into the kitchen beyond.

HOLLYHEAD

MARY HUCKLEBERRY

The others followed. Moments later Ada heard her soft and silky voice floating back into the outer pantry.

'My dear Mrs Beat'em, what an honour to meet you at last! The Duchess of Devon can't speak highly enough of your penguin-tongue sorbet.'

'Obliged, I'm sure.' Mrs Beat'em's voice sounded surprisingly friendly.

'Oh my! What a magnificent stove! But then a true culinary artist such as yourself deserves nothing less. I'm sure we all agree,' Nigellina continued.

Ada heard a strange gurgling noise and realized that this must be the sound of Mrs Beat'em giggling.

'You're too kind,' she said. 'The Inferno comes all the way from Florence. It has twelve ovens, twenty hobs and four roasting spits . . .'

While Mrs Beat'em began to demonstrate the many marvels of her stove to the visiting chefs, in the outer pantry Ada told Emily and Ruby all about Marylebone.

'Your lady's maid is a bear?' said Emily, her eyes wide with astonishment.

'Yes and I've only just found out,' said Ada.

'That explains a lot,' said Ruby thoughtfully.

'It does?' said Ada.

'Well, when we send meals upstairs, your maid always sends notes requesting honey,' Ruby replied. 'And often quince-marmalade sandwiches. She has lovely handwriting for a bear . . .' Ruby continued.

'And you say that she's in love?' Emily interrupted. 'How romantic! I'd love to paint her portrait.'

'The trouble is she's so shy that she can't bring herself to leave my rooms,' said Ada, 'and if we can't coax her out, she won't be able to marry General Simon Batholiver.'

'Well, if you can't get Marylebone to go to the general,' said Ruby, delicately attaching a fin to the tail of a sugar mermaid, 'perhaps you can ask the general to come to Marylebone?'

'Did someone just mention a general? I consider myself to be a general,' said a short man in a white military-style hat and jacket who'd just that minute entered the outer pantry from the kitchen garden. 'General in the kitchen, that is. Heston Harboil, experimental baker. I've come for—'

'Let me guess,' said Emily with a smile. 'The Great Ghastly-Gorm Bake Off.

HESTON HARBOIL

PUSHKIN

You'll find the others in the kitchen. Who's this?' She pointed to the extremely fat Muscovy duck that had just waddled in holding a leather bag in its beak.

'Oh, this is my assistant, Pushkin,*' said Heston Harboil. He took off his small wire-framed glasses and polished them on the hem of his jacket before returning them to his nose and peering closely at Ruby's mermaids.

'Sweet seaweed for the hair, I think,' he said, 'and . . . let me see . . .' He took his bag from Pushkin's beak, opened it and with a flourish produced a small glass test tube. 'Sugar cuttlefish — just a dusting to make those scales really shimmer. Here, let me show you . . .'

Ruby was entranced as Heston Harboil sprinkled the glittery powder on the tails of the icing-sugar mermaids, then took off his glasses once more and caught a ray of sunlight from the

Webbed Foot Notes

*Pushkin is a talented pastry chef who, as an ugly duckling, was taught in the Kremlin kitchens by a raspy-voiced imperial cook called Peter the Grate. Pushkin doesn't have teeth but does have a sweet-duck bill.

high window in one lens. Carefully he focused
the light, heating the powder and turning it into a
silvery liquid that covered the tails. Ruby gasped
with delight.

'Now for that hair . . .' Heston said.

'Let's leave them to it,' said Emily, taking Ada by the hand and leading her outside into the kitchen garden. The kitchen garden was where all the vegetables, fruit and herbs used in the kitchens of Ghastly-Gorm Hall were grown. Tiny tomatoes, odd-shaped cucumbers, giant marrows and monster pumpkins grew in raised beds, together with Cockney apples and pears and Glaswegian gooseberries. Next to the kitchen garden was the bedroom garden, where all the sweet-smelling flowers used in the bedrooms of Ghastly-Gorm Hall grew. Rambling roses, gambolling petunias and rampant pansies sprouted in profusion, flowering beside old meadow plants like Polly-go-lightly, bishop's slipper and mocking Simon. A gate at the end of the bedroom garden led into the drawing-room garden, which was really just a lawn with garden furniture laid out across it.

'You know, Ruby's got a point,' said Emily, stopping beside a Shoreditch orange-pippin tree and picking an apple. 'Can you send a message to General Batholiver?'

'*I* can't,' said Ada, her green eyes twinkling, 'but I know someone who can.'

Chapter Four

ipping the packet, Ada sprinkled some birdseed on the gravel path. They were standing by the gate to the drawing-room garden. Deckstools, chaises-foldings and swinging armchairs stood in large clusters around collapsible Chippendale tables on the neatly trimmed lawn.

A few moments later there was the sound of fluttering wings and a white dove swooped down and landed at Ada's feet. It had a small roll of paper tied around its leg. The dove began pecking at the birdseed.

'Can I borrow a pencil?' Ada asked Emily.

'Of course,' said Emily, who always wore a pencil attached to a ribbon around her neck. She slipped the ribbon over her head and handed Ada the pencil, then watched in fascination as

Ada gently scooped up the dove in her arms and untied the roll of paper from its leg.

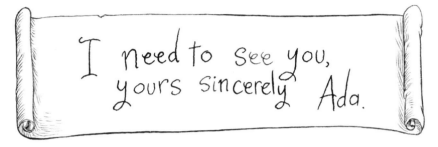

I need to see you,
yours sincerely Ada.

. . . she wrote in her best handwriting.

Emily held the dove while Ada tied the paper back on its leg, then let it go. The dove flapped up into the sky and flew off in the direction of the Back of Beyond Garden (Unfinished).

Just then Ada heard a familiar wheezing voice coming from the opposite end of the drawing-room garden. It was Maltravers.

'Hurry up, gentlemen,' he said in a sneering voice. 'I haven't got all day, and this furniture won't fold itself!'

Looking over the gate, Ada saw that Maltravers had the grooms from the hobby-horse stables

with him. As she and
Emily watched, the
grooms began folding
up the chairs
and tables and
stacking them
neatly against
the garden wall.
Maltravers
sat down in
a swinging
armchair
and
propped
his feet
up on
a deckstool. He pulled an extremely crumpled
newspaper from his pocket, unfolded it and began
to read.

'Chop-chop!' Maltravers voice sounded
from behind the copy of the *Observer of London*.

'I want the lawn completely cleared.'

'That's my father's newspaper!' said Ada indignantly. 'If he was here he'd be very cross at how creased Maltravers is making it.'

'Look,' said Emily, 'there's Arthur!'

Arthur Halford worked in the hobby-horse stables and was a member of the Attic Club, which met once a week in secret in the attics of Ghastly-Gorm Hall to share observations. Ada, Emily and William were also members, along with Ruby the outer-pantry maid and Kingsley the chimney caretaker. Kingsley was quite young to be chimney caretaker, but the last one had run off with one of Ada's previous governesses, Hebe Poppins.

Ada and Emily waved to Arthur, who put down the complicated chaise-folding he was wrestling with and trotted over to the gate.

'We've got to get all this lot cleared away ready for the Spiegel tent,' he said. 'It's where the Great Ghastly-Gorm Bake Off is going to take place, according to Maltravers, though it's the first any

of us grooms has heard about it.'

'Stop dawdling, Halford!' Maltravers called from behind Lord Goth's newspaper.

'I'd better get back to work,' said Arthur with a shrug. 'I'll see you both at the Attic Club later.'

Ada and Emily said goodbye, and had just turned away from the gate when the dove landed on it.

'What does it say?' said Emily, wide-eyed, as Ada unrolled the message.

Meet me by the fountain at ten to three ... and is there honey still for tea? Whimsy.

... Ada read.

'What does *that* mean?' said Emily.

'I'm not sure exactly,' said Ada. 'Lord Sydney is quite mysterious . . .'

'I can't wait to meet him!' said Emily.

✤

At ten minutes to three, Ada, Emily and her brother, William, who'd found his trousers, stood by the overly ornamental fountain. There was no sign of Lord Sydney Whimsy. William leaned back against a frowning stone goldfish and turned the colour of mossy marble.

'I wonder where he is,' Emily said, unfolding her stool and taking her watercolours out. 'Now, which one shall I paint today?' she murmured to herself as she looked up at the fountain. It was covered in statues — mermaids, mermen and mer-horses jostled for space with leaping dolphins and reclining sea gods; crowds of water babies clustered around sea-shells while groups of water teenagers skulked behind curling coral. There were so many statues that there was only room in the overly ornamental fountain for a tiny pool into which a thin dribble of water fell from the lip of a sulky-looking sea monster known as 'Mopey Dick'.

'I think . . . that one,' said Emily, opening her

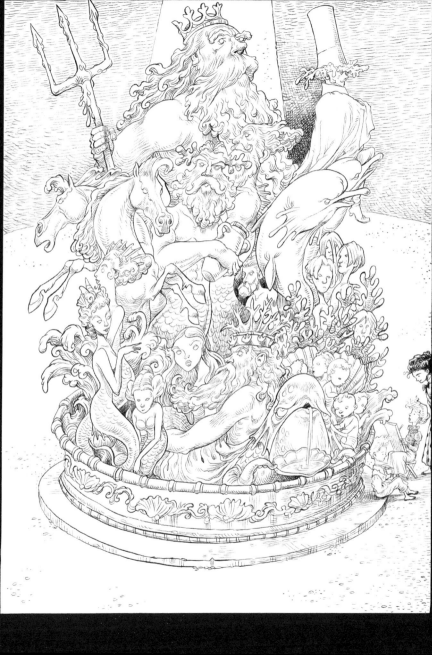

sketchbook and beginning to draw a merman in a long cloak and a tall hat fringed with seaweed who was perched on a dolphin.

'That's odd,' said Ada, looking at Emily's sketch, then back at the merman. 'I didn't think mermen wore top hats . . .'

'This one does!' said the statue. It got off the dolphin's back and climbed down the fountain towards them. As it did so, a cloud of white flour puffed up from its hat and shoulders.

'Lord Sydney!' exclaimed Ada. 'You

were here the whole time! How clever!'

Lord Sydney stepped down from the fountain and shook his cloak, then picked the seaweed from his hat. He smiled.

'Disguise is a useful tool in my line of work,' he said modestly, 'and flour is a useful tool for disguise. Anyway, I must say, you've captured quite a likeness, Miss Cabbage,' he continued, looking over Emily's shoulder at her drawing. 'You have quite a talent. But then so do you, William!'

William was staring at Lord Sydney, his mouth half open, clearly impressed.

'You must come and see me when you're older, William. I think you could have a very promising future. Talking of which, what does the future hold for your lady's maid, Miss Goth?'

'That's what I wanted to talk to you about,' Ada began.

Lord Sydney took her by the arm and they began to walk slowly round the overly ornamental fountain, arm in arm. Emily carried on painting while William stretched out at her feet and went a gravel colour. They were both listening intently.

'You see,' said Ada, 'your friend Simon's proposal brought back all sorts of memories for Marylebone. She says she loves him but she's just too nervous and frightened to leave my wardrobe.'

'Ruby wondered whether Simon could come here to Ghastly-Gorm Hall instead,' said Emily, without looking up from her painting.

'Ah, yes, Ruby the outer-pantry maid,' said Lord Sydney with a knowing smile. 'Very good at cake decoration, I understand. What a talented group of young people you Attic Clubbers are!'

'You know about the Attic Club?' said William, sitting up. 'But it's secret!'

'Your secret is safe with me,' Lord Sydney assured him, 'but two bears in your wardrobe, Miss Goth? I fear it would never work.'

'But there must be something we can do,' said Ada.

Two doves came fluttering down and landed on Lord Sydney's shoulders, one on either side. There was a short pause while he read their messages and sent them off with replies.

'I am rather busy with this fete just at the moment, arranging tent deliveries, painting stagecoaches, organizing village bands, not to mention other matters . . .' he said mysteriously. Then he turned to Ada and patted her hand. 'But I'll give the problem some thought. Now, if you'll excuse me, Miss Goth, I'm due in the village for some dancing lessons and I still have to weave my straw skirt . . .'

Chapter Five

For the rest of the afternoon Ada and Emily explored the wild and overgrown Back of Beyond Garden (Unfinished). It was Ada's favourite part of the grounds and the area that the famous landscape architect, Metaphorical Smith, hadn't quite got round to finishing. It had the Secret Garden at its heart and beyond that, through a little door, the Even-More-Secret Garden.

This was where Ada and Emily were growing the more unusual plants they'd discovered in Metaphorical Smith's 'Greenhouse of Harmony'.* They

Webbed Foot Notes

*The Greenhouse of Harmony was built by Metaphorical Smith for growing delicate plants from very hot countries. He didn't believe in throwing stones.

rather lost track of the time, and it was getting dark when they finally got back to the house. They decided to avoid the kitchens just in case they were still crowded with cooks, and entered the west wing instead, through the Byzantine windows of the Venetian terrace.

'Who'd have thought an Easter-egg plant could smell of chocolate?' said Emily.

'I'll see you tomorrow for breakfast,' said Ada, waving goodbye to Emily at the foot of the staircase.

'We can repot the purple geranium,' Emily called back as she walked across the large marble hall towards the east wing.

TULGEY WOOD TREE

EASTER EGG PLANT

THE PURPLE GERANIUM OF CAIRO

Ada climbed the stairs to her rooms on the second floor of the west wing. She wished she could slide up the banister the way Lucy Borgia did, but her governess had said that Ada wasn't quite ready for levitation lessons yet. Ada opened the door to her extremely large bedroom and stepped inside to see her supper waiting for her on the more-than-occasional table. She sat down and as she lifted the large silver-domed lid there was a smell of bonfires and a cloud of soft smoke billowed up into the air. Ada looked down to see a little glass teapot with a nightingale for a spout bubbling over a candle. Steam poured out through the bird's beak in a melodic and haunting whistle. Next to the teapot there was a bowl and a spoon resting on a bed of straw, and a little card . . .

Ada poured the soup into the bowl and scooped up a warm, scented spoonful. She took a sip. It was the most delicious soup she'd ever tasted!

When Ada had finished it, she realized that she still had Emily's pencil around her neck. She picked up the card, turned it over and wrote . . .

Dear Mr Harboil,
your soup was delicious –
it gave me a beautiful sad
feeling like the end of summer.
yours sincerely, Ada.

Then she placed the card next to the empty bowl
and glass teapot, blew out the candle and put back
the silver lid. She glanced over at the Dalmatian
divan and saw that Marylebone had laid out her
black velvet cape.

'I hope you're feeling better,' she called to the
closed wardrobe door and heard a low growl in
reply. 'I've left a copy of my father's book on the
mantelpiece for you.'

Ada put on her cape, picked up her fencing
umbrella and went up to the rooftops.

✻

It was a beautiful, clear night and the not-quite
full moon shone down on the ornamental
chimneys, which cast slanting shadows across
the slate tiles.

Ada glanced up at the window in the small
turret at the top of
Ghastly-Gorm Hall's
central dome. It was
dark, so Lucy Borgia
hadn't got up yet.

Just then she saw
a sinister shape pass
across the face
of the moon.
As Ada
watched,
the
shape
grew
larger in
the sky.

It was a hot-air balloon! In the sudden flare of the burner Ada saw three figures, dark-eyed and white-faced, staring down from the balloon's basket. One of the figures leaned over the side as the balloon approached the rooftops and called down to Ada.

'Little girl, little girl,' he said, 'is this the Hall of Ghastly-Gorm, by any chance?'

'Home of the famous Poet of the Bicycle, Lord Goth?' said one of his companions, adjusting his spectacles.

'Yes, it is,' said Ada taking a step back and clutching her umbrella tightly as the balloon came lower, passing over the four chimney pots of 'The Brothers Grim and the Sisters Jolly'. 'Lord Goth is my father.'

'So you must be the little Goth girl,' said the third passenger in a soft, lilting voice. She wore a large powdered wig and had a black silk scarf wound around her neck.

Up close, Ada could see that the basket of the

balloon was heavily laden with groceries of all sorts — long loaves of bread, bottles of golden oil, cured sausages tied with criss-crossing string. What didn't fit inside the basket was strapped to the sides or hung down in sacks on the end of the ropes.

'Didier Dangle and Gerard Dopplemousse, Grocers of the Night,' said the man in the spectacles.

He appeared to be wearing a wig too, though Ada couldn't be sure. 'And this is our balloonist, Madame Grand Gousier.' The three of them nodded stiffly, and none of them smiled as they stared coldly down at her. The balloon hovered above 'Old Smokey' and Ada heard a snuffling sound coming from inside the basket.

'We have deliveries to make,' said Didier Dangle, 'for the contestants in the Bake Off of Greatness . . .'

He glanced down at the copy of the *Observer of London* that he held in his hand. 'They are the foremost cooks in the land, we understand.'

'Heston Harboil is certainly very good,' said Ada. 'I'm not sure about the others, but they all seem very keen . . .'

'They sound *delicious*,' said Madame Grand Gousier, turning up the burner and sending a jet of yellow flame up into the balloon, which began to rise once more.

'We will deliver our groceries to the . . . tradesmen's entrance –' Gerard Dopplemousse winced as he said the word 'tradesmen's' – 'and be on our way. *Bonne nuit*, Mademoiselle Goth,' he said stiffly.

Ada watched the balloon sail off, over the rooftops, past the dome and down towards the east wing. She lost sight of it as it came down low over the kitchens on the other side of the house.

She turned back to see a dove had landed on the rooftop beside her. She read the message it had brought.

Dear Ada,
Lord Whimsy has invited me punting on the lake by moonlight.
We shall resume our lessons tomorrow.
Lucy

Ada couldn't help feeling a little disappointed. She had been looking forward to her umbrella-fencing lesson, and besides, she was curious to know what her governess would make of the Grocers of the Night. Ada didn't like the look of them.

She climbed up on to 'Antony and Cleopatra', which was one of her favourite chimneys. Ada liked the stone sphinx supporting the chimney stacks. Just as she was about to tiptoe along its back, a sooty head popped up out of 'Antony'.

'Thought I'd find you here,' it said.

Ada blushed. It was Kingsley the chimney caretaker.

He climbed out of the chimney and folded the two brushes attached to his back, sending a cloud of soot into the air. Then he took out a spotted handkerchief, wiped the grime off his face and hands and sat down next to Ada on the sphinx's back.

'How's the Greenhouse of Harmony? Discovered any interesting plants recently?' he asked.

'We took a cutting from the tulgeywood tree,' said Ada,

'and it seems to be growing really well. I think it likes it when Emily and I talk to it . . .'

'That's strange,' said Kingsley.

'Not really – we compliment it on its crinkly leaves and knobbly trunk . . .'

'No, not the tree,' said Kingsley, pointing across the rooftops at 'Old Smokey' – '*that.*'

Ada looked. A trail of smoke was curling up out of the crooked chimney.

'Old Smokey hasn't been used for years,' said Kingsley. 'I think I'd better investigate.'

'Can I come?' said Ada excitedly. 'Where does Old Smokey's

chimney lead to?'

Kingsley got slowly to his feet and scratched his head thoughtfully. 'If I remember correctly, it leads to an old furnace,' he said, and his eyes narrowed, 'in the Whine Cellars.'

Kingsley was even better than Ada at sliding down banisters, and in no time at all they were down in the great marble-floored entrance

GRACE, GRACE
AND
GRACE.

hall of Ghastly-Gorm Hall. As they made their way past the groups of statues that littered the enormous space, Ada found herself looking extra closely at each one in case they turned out to be Lord Sydney in disguise. Just around the corner from the three pear-shaped Graces that, in the

moonlight streaming down from the dome, Ada
could tell weren't anyone in disguise, they came
to the entrance to the Whine Cellars, where Ada
had bumped into Maltravers earlier that day. It
was a small arch-shaped doorway through which
narrow stone steps descended into the darkness.
The carved face of a bald Irish wolfhound looked
down at Ada from the centre of the arch. Kingsley
took a candle from the iron holder on the wall
and held it up above his head.

Ada avoided the wolfhound's baleful stare as she followed Kingsley down the stone steps.

The damp walls glistened in the candlelight, and cobwebs like grey tapestries wafted above their heads as they passed by.

At the bottom of the steps, Kingsley and Ada paused and looked around. In the gloom, they

ABBA THE MINOTAUR

saw row after row of stone shelves stacked with dusty bottles stretching off into the distance, with narrow pathways between them. It reminded Ada of the labyrinth her friend the Siren Sesta had told her about, where Abba* the depressed Swedish minotaur lived.

Webbed Foot Notes

*Abba the Swedish Minotaur likes pickled herring, knitted jumpers and long walks in the rain. He composes annoyingly catchy songs on his Scandinavian lyre.

Kingsley pointed down one passage where there was a faint chink of light just visible. 'The furnace room must be down there,' he whispered.

Ada followed him past the shelves of dusty bottles. She ran a finger across a label as she went by.

Ada didn't like the sound of that.

Suddenly echoing through the cellars came a sound that made Ada and Kingsley stop in their tracks.

Long, low, and mournful, it was the unmistakable sound of a whine.

Chapter Six

uddenly, from behind them, two enormous poodles appeared, one black as midnight, the other a ghostly white.

Yapping and whining, they hurtled down the aisle between the stacks, their claws scritter-scratching on the flagstones. Nimble as a mouse up a grandfather clock, Kingsley jumped up on to a stone shelf and, shooting out an arm, pulled Ada up to join him. The two poodles didn't even pause as they dashed past, their pom-pom tails swishing and their whines growing more agitated. At the end of the aisle they came to a halt and began scratching at a large metal door from beneath which a chink of light was escaping. Whines filled the gloomy vaults of the cellars. Two huge bottles of champagne lay side by side on the shelf next to Ada and Kingsley, and they

had to be careful not to send them crashing to the floor.

'Belle, my Belle! And Sebastian, *mon chéri!*' came Madame Grand Gousier's soft, tinkling voice, and the door opened just wide enough for the poodles to slip inside. 'Your crêpes are ready!' they heard, as the metal door clanged shut.

'Who was that?' said Kingsley in astonishment. 'And what are they doing in the old furnace room?'

'That was Madame Grand Gousier the balloonist – those poodles must belong to her,' said Ada. 'She's one of the grocers delivering supplies for the bake off. At least that's what they *said* they were doing . . .'

Just then the door opened again and Maltravers backed out. 'Let me know if there's anything else you need,' he wheezed, 'to make your stay more—' The door slammed in his face, interrupting him. '. . . comfortable.'

Maltravers turned and hurried away, muttering beneath his breath.

'He's definitely up to something, and I don't like it,' said Ada, after he had gone. 'I wish my father was here.'

'Me too,' said Kingsley, 'but until he gets back

from his book tour, the Attic Club will have to keep a close eye on things.'

They climbed down from the wine stack and crept, as quietly as they could, out of the Whine Cellars and into the entrance hall.

'We'll talk about all this at the Attic Club tomorrow,' said Ada, as they walked past the statue of the three Graces in the entrance hall. 'In the meantime I'll ask William to follow Maltravers everywhere – he's very good at not being seen.'

'Oh, I wouldn't bother,' said the fourth Grace, suddenly stepping down from the other three on the plinth.

'Lord Sydney!' said Ada. 'You made me jump.'

'Apologies, Miss Goth,' said Lord Sydney, removing his dust sheet with a flourish, 'but leave Maltravers to me. I'll make a full report to your father when he gets back from the Lake District.'

He took a small rolled-up note from his pocket. 'Right now he's sheltering from a thunderstorm beneath a gorse

balloon was heavily laden with groceries of all sorts – long loaves of bread, bottles of golden oil, cured sausages tied with criss-crossing string. What didn't fit inside the basket was strapped to the sides or hung down in sacks on the end of the ropes.

'Didier Dangle and Gerard Dopplemousse, Grocers of the Night,' said the man in the spectacles.